W9-BHY-988

The Bicycle Garden

by Walter Williams

The Bicycle Garden by Walter Williams
Published by Fernwood and Hedges Books (2013)
First Edition
Library of Congress Control Number: 2012955229
ISBN: 978-0-9890698-0-9

For my children

Timka and Dasha decided to grow a bicycle in their backyard garden.

Using magic seeds, they tilled and watered the soil until...

...handlebars sprouted out of the ground.

Soon, they had a bicycle with a comfy seat and sturdy frame that they delighted in riding around the neighborhood.

The next morning, much to their surprise, Timka and Dasha discovered their bicycle had grown.

In fact, their bicycle grew so fast that by the afternoon the handlebars were in the clouds.

Timka and Dasha planted more seeds.

But that bicycle, too, grew out of reach.

So they planted...

...and planted...

...and planted, until their backyard was full of giant tires and frames that touched the sky.

With no more seeds and no more room left to plant, Timka and Dasha were in despair.

But then they spotted what appeared to be two bicycles hidden among the giant tires and spokes.

Timka and Dasha scaled the vines to the bicycles and set them free.

The next morning, Timka and Dasha were happy to see their bicycles were neither too big nor too small...

...but just right.

The End

CPSIA information can be obtained
at www.ICGtesting.com
Printed in the USA
LVIW02n1502311013
359479LV00022B/255

[7]